A TALE of TWO DRAGONS

Geraldine McCaughrean

Peter Malone

Andersen Press

The Kingdoms of Arbor and Pomosa stood back-to-back. Each had a castle bristling with guards.

Arbor was plush with trees in every shade of green: woods and orchards full of mushrooms, fruit and birds.

Pomosa was rich too, golden with wheat fields, silver lakes and creamy, milkful cows. A high thorn-hedge parted the two territories.

Sometimes, it's true, the people of Pomosa would look across at the plush forests and say, "If only we had trees. It is hard to make wheat-flour into loaves without wood to heat the bread ovens."

And the children heard them say it.

Sometimes the people
of Arbor would look
across at Pomosa
and say, "If only we
had wheat and rice
we could make into
pies and porridge
and pancakes."

And the children heard
them say it.

If only the thieving children of Pomosa had not found a way through the hedge and gathered fallen branches and dragged them home for firewood, to please their mothers.

But they did.

If only the thieving children of Arbor had not come creeping at night to cut corn and milk cows and tiptoe home to surprise the grown-ups with sheaves of grain and buckets of milk.

But they did.

As the thieves became more and more daring, the two Kings grew more and more annoyed, "Post guards with swords and torches! This stealing must stop!"

But either the guards were lazy or they looked the other way, because – do you know what? – not a single child thief was caught or thrown into a dungeon.

The Kings threw tantrums and shook their fists at one another.

"A dragon! Find me a dragon!" the King of Arbor told his ambassadors.

"The biggest you can find!"

The ambassadors took ship for China to seek out a dragon.

Much to their surprise, one agreed to come, in return for a
wage of plums, pears and pine cones.

Watched from the battlements of both castles, she stepped out along
the Arbor Highway, her scales catching the sunlight. A creature of such

pure power that the King of Arbor dared not go down to greet her.

"Guard my country!" he shouted down. "Kill any Pomosa thieves!"

The King of Pomosa sulked and stamped, "I want a dragon! I need a dragon to guard my country from that ugly great beast!"

Ambassadors were sent to China and, much to their surprise, a dragon was found who agreed to come in return for ginger, gooseberries and goldfish.

Watched from the battlements of both castles he came striding along the Pomosa Highway. "Fearful!" murmured the men. "Huge!" whispered the women. "But it's so beautiful!" they all agreed.

Both nations gasped in amazement.

Neither dragon noticed. They were busy eyeing each other, scales rippling. The colours pulsed in their arched backs. Smoke trickled out of nostrils and ears. There was no reading the thoughts behind their glittering eyes.

Children hid behind their mothers' skirts. There would be no more thieving of wood or wheat.

But bakers still needed wood to heat their ovens, and winter nights are cold without logs for the fire. Woodsmen need bread and porridge, and growing children need milk.

From their rooftops, the people watched the dragons patrol. So exquisite, so exotic... so terrifying. As one walked West, the other ambled East, with only a thorn-hedge between them. (Naturally, each country thought its own dragon was the best.)

"We must have timber!" said the King of Pomosa.
"Order my dragon to kill that monster next-door!"
"We must have milk and bread," said the King of Arbor.
"Tell my dragon to kill that creature next-door."

Dragons are noble beasts. Was it their good manners
that kept them from refusing to fight?
The she-dragon reared up on her
hind legs. The he-dragon stood tall.
No one could tell what they
were thinking.

They fought.

"Stop them!" cried the people of Arbor. "We didn't want this."
Dragon-fire blazed.
"Stop them!" cried the people of Pomosa. "We never asked for this!"

But the dragons fought on, ears torn and snouts bleeding, coughing up
black smoke.
"Stop them!"

But the Kings watched with snarling glee.

"If mine wins, your kingdom belongs to me!"

The dragons fought until they could fight no more.

Both toppled at the same moment and lay,

"If mine wins, your kingdom belongs to me!"

long necks overlapping, their fire out.
Their blazing colours had faded to grey.

Then people ran from
their houses.

They brought
milk and pine cones, gooseberries
and hot water. They brought herbs and honey to
spread on the wounds and stroked the big heads.

They plucked thorns out of soft, dragon armpits.

"He was so beautiful. He was *our* dragon."

"She was so brave. She was *ours*."

A long, long tongue slithered out between
the she-dragon's lips and licked a nearby snout. The he-dragon
opened his grey eyes. A strangely dragonish voice murmured,
"We have done what we came to do. Now they understand."

The two kingdoms of
Arbor and Pomosa
stand shoulder-to-
shoulder.
There is a line
somewhere
parting the two
countries, but it is
hard to see: the baby
dragons' tails scuff it
out as they play. And
their parents lie
back-to-back feeling
each other's warmth.

There are no kings now. Somehow no one could remember what kings were for, and sent theirs away to find out. And since everyone needs bread and wood, birdsong and honey, apples and milk, the people freely come and go, to and fro every other day or so.

But on Dragon Day, they do nothing but dance.